Will A Clownfish Make You Giggle?

Will A Clownfish Make You Giggle?

Answers To Some Very Fishy Questions

by Kay Dokken
Illustrated by Victoria Marcellan–Allen

Aqua Quest Publications, Inc. ■ New York

Library of Congress Cataloging-in-Publication Data
Dokken, Kay.
    Will a clownfish make you giggle? : answers to some very fishy
questions / by Kay Dokken ; illustrated by Victoria Marcellan-Allen.
        p.   cm.
    Summary: Plays on the "fishy" names of twelve marine animals and
tells where these names come from while teaching the natural history
of the animals and their habitats.
    ISBN 1-881652-07-6 (casebound)
    1. Marine fauna—Miscellanea—Juvenile literature. 2. Marine
ecology—Miscellanea—Juvenile literature. [1. Marine animals.
2. Marine ecology. 3. Ecology.] I. Marcellan-Allen, Victoria,
ill. II. Title.
QL122.2.D64 1995
591.92—dc20   95-4772
                                                  CIP

Distributed to the book trade by National Book Network.
800-462-6420; 301-459-3366

Printed in Hong Kong
10 9 8 7 6 5 4 3 2 1

For Quenton and John,
true adventurers.
—K.D.

For Ricardo y Timoteo,
precious memories that will
live on with your family.
—V.A.

WILL A CLOWNFISH MAKE YOU GIGGLE?

With his painted face and bright stripes, the clownfish looks like a jolly clown.

This clever little fish gets help from the poisonous anemone to trap his food and to keep him safe from other fish. Protected by a mucus coating, the clownfish hides from his hungry enemies by snuggling safely among the anemone's deadly tentacles.

When a fish swims too close, the anemone stings and traps it. The trapped animal becomes dinner for both the clownfish and the anemone.

Although the clownfish may not make you laugh, he may be giggling at all the fish who cannot make a meal out of him!

As if by magic, a crown slowly appears on the head of the queen angelfish as she grows up.

This colorful angelfish lives in the best palaces of warm, shallow waters near coral reefs. The small animals she feeds on are easy to find there. She turns right side up, sideways, and even upside down to pluck food from the cracks in the reefs.

Each queen chooses a special area around a reef as her kingdon. She almost always reigns alone as she swims slowly and gracefully around her home.

Wearing a jewelled crown and a robe of beautiful colors, the queen angelfish is the picture of royalty.

CAN A PARROTFISH FLY?

Like a parrot, this fish has bold colors. He has teeth that are shaped like a beak.

The parrotfish noisily bites off pieces of crusty coral with his strong beak. He grinds the coral with special teeth in the back of his throat. Algae that grows on the coral and the tiny animals that build the coral, called polyps, are his food. The ground up coral is returned to the sea as sand.

Some parrotfish make a clear bubble, or cocoon, to sleep in at night. Scientists think he uses the bubble to hide his scent from predators who are looking for a nighttime snack.

This underwater parrot swims. He cannot fly.

HOW SWEET IS A JELLYFISH?

The jellyfish is named for her soft, almost clear body. Athough the word "fish" is in her name, this animal is not a fish at all. The jellyfish has no eyes or bones. Her large head is called a bell, and her body is made mostly of water.

The jellyfish has tentacles instead of fins like a fish has, and some of the tentacles sting. The stinging tentacles are used to catch food and to keep away enemies. The jellyfish cannot tell the difference between an enemy and a person, so don't swim too close to one.

Watch the jellyfish from far away. Its sting is not very sweet.

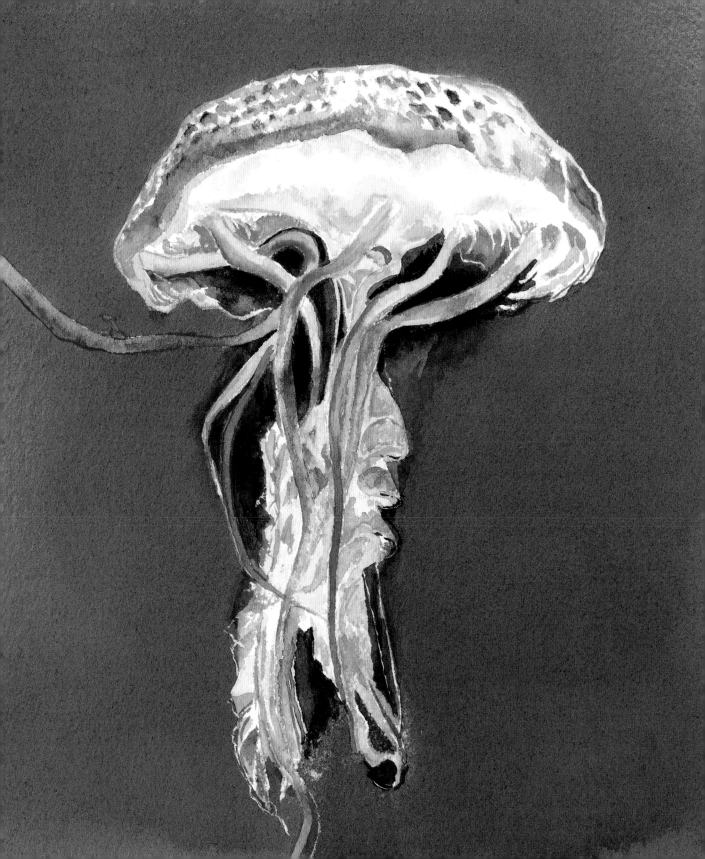

WILL A LEMON SHARK MAKE YOU PUCKER?

The lemon shark is a large, grumpy-looking fish.

The yellow color on the sides of his body gives this shark his name. He is shaped like a submarine. He swims fast but cannot stop quickly or back up.

His rough skin feels like sandpaper. He has no eyelids, so he never blinks. He stares all the time.

His mouth is turned down in a sour snarl. It is filled with sharp, pointed teeth. There are rows and rows of extra teeth in his strong jaw. When a tooth is lost, a new one replaces it.

If you saw a lemon shark swimming your way, wouldn't your face pucker?

CAN A FIDDLER CRAB PLAY A TUNE?

The male fiddler crab uses his large claw and his long legs to make music by the seaside.

To find a mate he drums on the ground with his big claw and makes a honking sound by rubbing his legs together. The noise he makes is his special melody. A female fiddler crab hears his tune and finds the fiddler.

To scare other creatures away from his burrow, the male fiddler crab waves his huge claw in the air. Except for his mate, he does not want any other animals fiddling around his home.

Indeed, the fiddler crab really can play a merry tune!

DOES A BLUE-RINGED OCTOPUS WEAR RINGS?

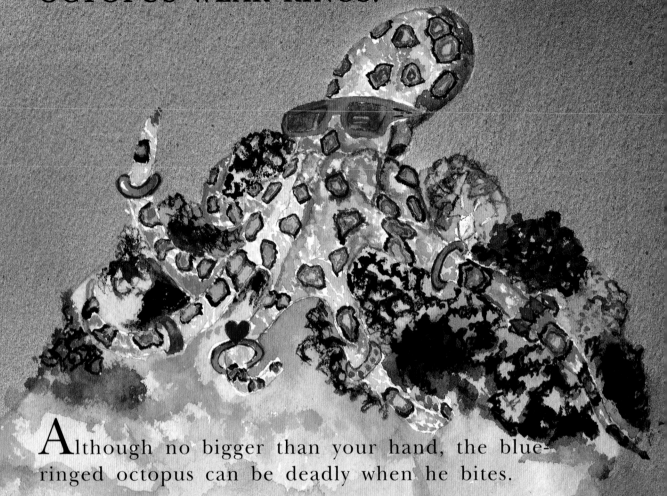

Although no bigger than your hand, the blue-ringed octopus can be deadly when he bites.

He is shy and would rather be left alone. He hides by changing his skin color to match the rocks or seabed around him. When scared, he shoots out a dark cloud of ink. The ink blocks an attacker from seeing or smelling the octopus while he jets away to safety.

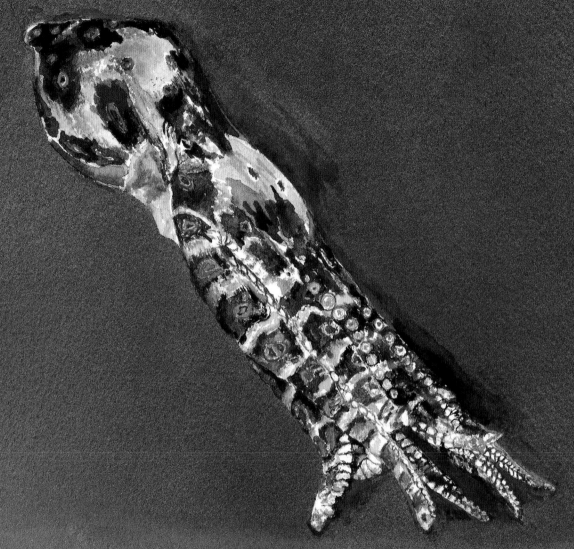

Eight limber arms are used to feel and taste. Suction cups on the bottom of his arms help the soft, boneless animal hold onto rocks and food.

The poisonous blue-ringed octopus is covered with many pretty blue rings. But let's not look too closely!

HOW MANY RIDDLES DOES THE RIDLEY TURTLE KNOW?

The ridley turtle has a sharp beak instead of teeth and strong flippers instead of feet. This turtle almost never leaves the sea.

When it is time for the female to lay eggs, she swims a long way to return to the same beach where she was hatched. She crawls out of the water and digs a hole for a nest. There she lays her eggs, covers them with sand, and returns to the sea. The sun warms the eggs in their sandy nest. When the baby turtles, called hatchlings, poke their way out of the eggs, they quickly scoot into the sea.

So the ridley turtle knows one riddle that no one else can answer: How does the mother turtle know just where to go lay her eggs?

CAN A PISTOL SHRIMP SHOOT?

POP! SNAP! CRACK! The pistol shrimp gets his name from the sharp snapping sound he makes with his large claw.

The little pistol shrimp is only one or two inches long, but he is one of the noisiest creatures in the ocean. Even people on the beach can hear this shrimp's "pistol" pop!

The shrimp uses the sound of his popping claw to chase away predators and to stun his prey. If the pistol shrimp loses the large claw, his other one soon grows big to replace it, and a small claw slowly grows to replace the missing one.

If you were a tiny pistol shrimp in a very large ocean, wouldn't you POP! SNAP! CRACK! your claw to sound big?

DOES A SQUIRRELFISH EAT NUTS?

The squirrelfish likes to rest in dark holes in the coral reef during the day.

When the sunlight dims, he swims out of his hiding place to feed on small animals. He has very large eyes that allow him to see well in the dark.

The scales on a squirrelfish have sharp edges. He has stiff, sharp spines on his cheek and on the fin on his back. To warn other fish to stay away, he raises the fin and makes clicking sounds.

The squirrelfish doesn't eat nuts, but he hides in a hole like a squirrel does.

The porcupinefish has sharp spines like a porcupine's quills.

When he feels safe, the spines on this fish lay flat against his body. When an enemy comes near, the porcupinefish sucks in water and swells up like a balloon. His spines poke out all over, making him look like a big, round pin cushion. He knows most of his enemies won't try to eat a fish covered with pins.

I'm sure the porcupinefish is glad to have lots of prickly spines to protect him.

CAN A SEA HORSE RUN A RACE?

The sea horse wears a second skeleton on the outside. This crusty, outer skeleton protects him from his enemies.

Although he is a fish, he swims very poorly. Most of his time is spent holding onto a plant with his curly tail. He dines on tiny animals that swim near him. He sucks food into his long, toothless mouth like a vacuum cleaner.

Instead of laying her eggs in the water, the mother sea horse lays her eggs in a pouch on the father's belly. When the eggs hatch, the father pushes the babies out into the water.

The sea horse does not swim fast. He is much too slow to race.

GLOSSARY

Algae. Plants found in or near water, which have no true flower, root, stem or leaf. They may be any size from very small to very large. Some fish eat algae.

Anemone. An animal which has many tentacles that can sting and capture food. Anemones are found in all the oceans. Many anemones look like flowers, but they are actually meat-eating animals.

Burrow. A hole in the ground dug by an animal and used for shelter. Many marine animals live in burrows made in the ocean floor. The fiddler crab makes his burrow in the sandy beach beside the ocean.

Cocoon. A protective covering. The parrotfish makes his cocoon of mucus which oozes from his skin.

Coral. The tiny animals, called polyps, which build their homes of calcium and other minerals taken from seawater. Corals form colonies, or groups, to make coral reefs.

Coral reef. A large group of polyps and the homes built by them which together form a rock-like mass in warm, shallow seas.

Mucus. Thick, gluey slime that covers the skin of most marine animals. It protects their skin and makes it easier for them to swim through the water.

Pouch. A pocket or bag on the stomach of some animals which is used to carry their young.

Predator. An animal that captures and eats other animals.

Prey. An animal hunted and eaten by another animal.

Quill. A sharp, hollow spine on an animal.

Scientist. A person who knows a lot about science. Marine scientists study the oceans and all the plants and animals that live there.

Skeleton. 1) The bones inside an animal that support its shape. 2) The very tough, crusty outer covering of an animal.

Spine. A stiff, sharp-pointed outgrowth on animals or plants.

Tentacle. A long and thin bendable arm that is used for feeling, eating, moving or holding onto things.

About the Author

Kay Dokken discovered the fascinating world of the ocean after moving to Corpus Christi, Texas from the dry plains of west Texas in the early 1970's. Inspired by her marine-biologist husband and her own love of the underwater world, Kay's book evolved from teaching her young son about the marine environment.

About the Illustrator

Vicki Marcellan-Allen is an Addy Award-winning artist who works as a designer and illustrator. She lives with her husband, son and daughter in Corpus Christi, Texas.

Distributed to the book trade by:
National Book Network, Inc.
4720-A Boston Way, Lanham, MD 20706
Telephone (800) 462-6420; Fax (301) 459-2118